D1217591

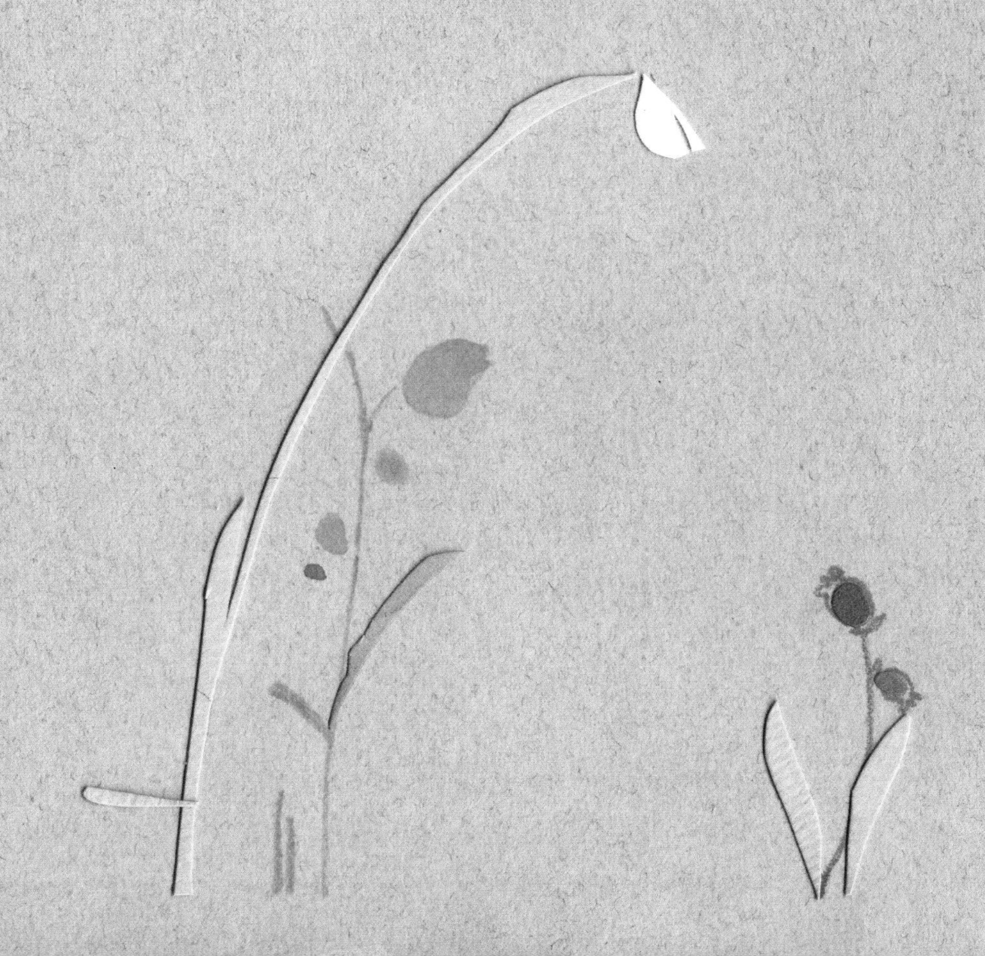

Thanks to the elders, for their wisdom.
—Pilar López Ávila

For the three artists, the beautiful flowers: Gemma, Marta, and Neus.
—Zuzanna Celej

This book is printed on **Stone Paper** that is **Silver Cradle to Cradle Certified®**.

Cradle to Cradle™ is one of the most demanding ecological certification systems, awarded to products that have been conceived and designed in an ecologically intelligent way.

Cuento de Luz™ became a **Certified B Corporation** in 2015. The prestigious certification is awarded to companies that use the power of business to solve social and environmental problems and meet higher standards of social and environmental performance, transparency, and accountability.

With a Butterfly's Wings

Calle Claveles, 10 | Pozuelo de Alarcón | 28223 | Madrid | Spain
www.cuentodeluz.com
Original title in Spanish: *Con alas de mariposa*
English translation by Jon Brokenbrow
ISBN: 978-84-18302-59-6
1st printing
Printed in PRC by Shanghai Cheng Printing Company, July 2021, print number 1840-6

With a Butterfly's Wings

By Pilar López Ávila

Illustrated by Zuzanna Celej

It was my grandma who taught me to listen to the songs of the birds.

She would say, "Listen. I can hear a mockingbird."

Or, "The blue herons have arrived!"

My grandma, who wove with brightly colored thread, would sit in the garden.

“You see those sparrows? The female has brown feathers, but the male has a mask and a bib, and he shows them off to her.”

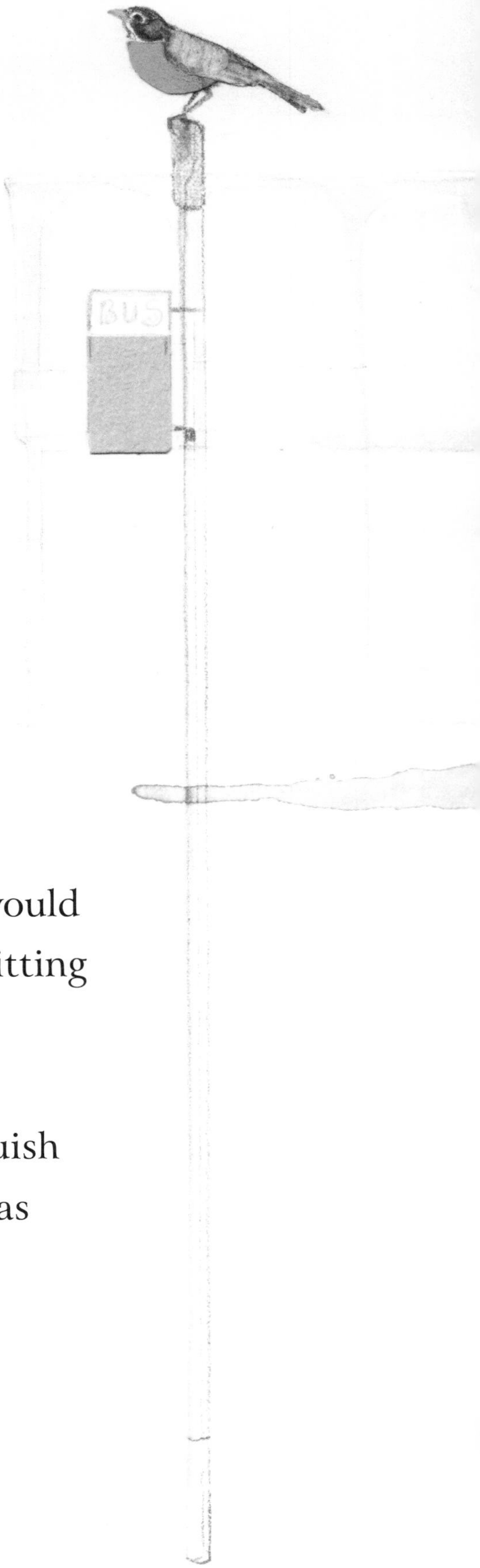

On February days, walking to school, she would say to me, "Can you hear the robin? He's sitting on that pole!"

And I would look for it, learning to distinguish his song from the rumble of the city that was slowly waking up.

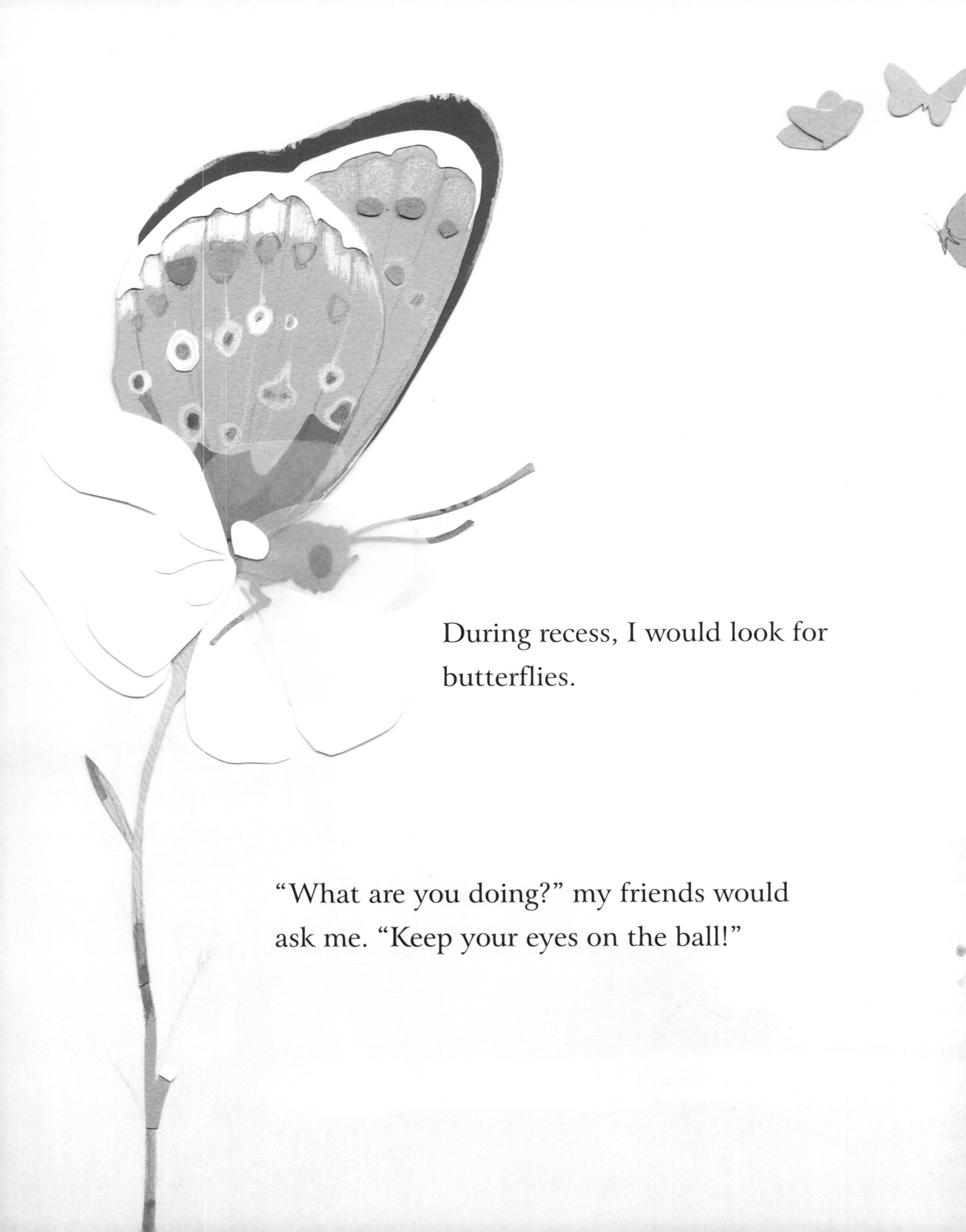

During recess, I would look for butterflies.

"What are you doing?" my friends would ask me. "Keep your eyes on the ball!"

And I would answer, "I just saw a little girl dressed in sky blue pass by!"

Then I would go home, and I'd tell my grandma everything I had seen.

She'd say to me, "This afternoon, we're going to look for the finches."

Holding hands, we would walk into the woods, and we would quietly watch as the birds built their nest among the branches.

Then they would flutter down onto the thistles, and we would gaze in wonder at the deep red color of their feathers.

"Grandma, it looks like you wove them with your red thread!" I'd say. And we would chuckle to ourselves quietly.

The first birds to arrive from the south were the swallows. And my grandma would say to me, "Their backs are cobalt blue, and their throats are cinnamon-colored."

Then the swifts would arrive, with their dark feathers and dazzling aerobatics. They would dive and soar into the sky, seeming to never touch the ground.

"At night, they sleep in the air!" my grandma would say. I thought it was amazing that they could sleep so close to the stars.

My grandma would tell me the names of all the flowers. Like the exquisite magnolias, which accompanied us on our strolls in the springtime.

But I preferred the humbler flowers, because they were the most beautiful.

The lilies.

The swamp azalea.

The bellflowers, which looked like the thimble Grandma used when she sewed with her colorful threads.

Nobody believed that it was my grandma who'd taught me these things. They would say to me, "It's impossible that you know so much about birds and butterflies and flowers." But it didn't bother me. I wanted to be just like her.

My grandma would tell me secrets:
"The hummingbirds make their nests out of moss and spiderwebs."

Sometimes we would walk
through the meadows to watch the
monarch butterflies gathering.

Then we would kneel down and look for four-leaf clovers. We would be so happy when we found one, because it was a sign of good luck.

I took everything in.
I saw a small bird of prey swooping through the sky. It was a kestrel.

I surprised a bluebird flying
into a hole in an old tree,
and I thought, "That's where
his nest is."

What I loved the best was to snuggle down in my bed and listen to the mysterious owls, imagining them camouflaged in a tree trunk.

"Grandma!" sang an owl, even though she couldn't hear it anymore.

Because my grandma was very old by now, and could hardly hear, hardly see, and hardly move at all.

But she said to me, "The day it's my turn to go, I'll fly around you first."

That day I was in the schoolyard, looking at something or other. Maybe it was a beautiful green-and-yellow butterfly.

A swallow appeared and flew several times around my head.

At first, I didn't realize it, but then I remembered. I remembered what she'd said to me.

And I knew it was her.

My grandma taught me the names of the butterflies.
Of the wildflowers.
She taught me to watch the birds in flight.

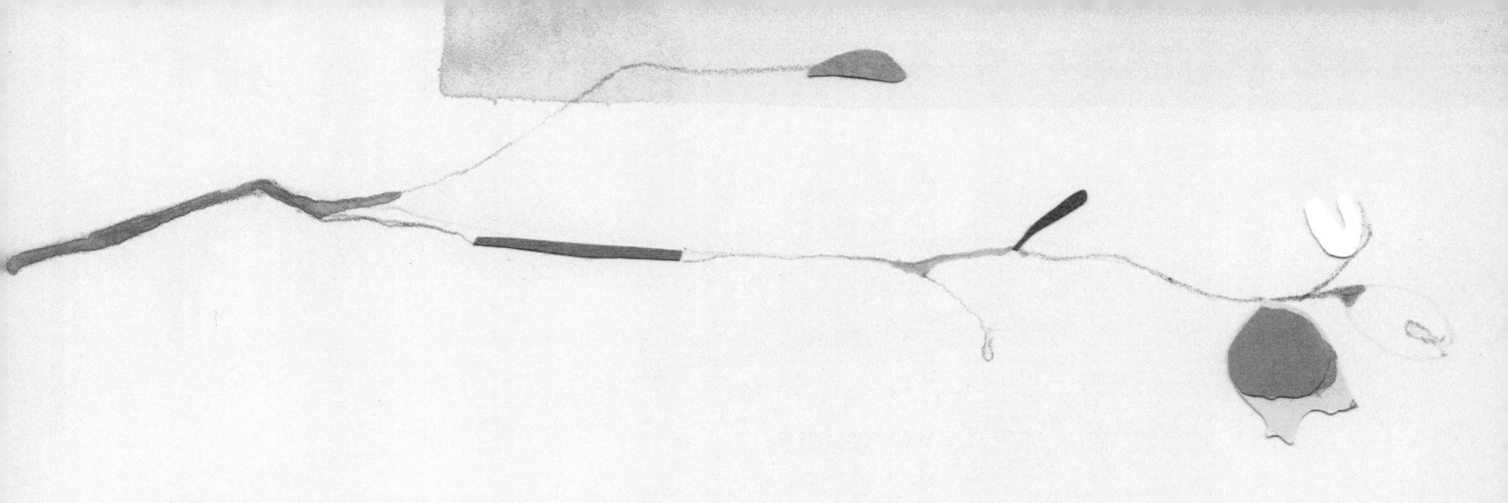

And when it's my turn to fly, I'll fly with a butterfly's wings.